Ty Catches a Dragon

To
Connor

Don Frederickson
09/22/2018

Books by
DON FREDERICKSON

THIEF FOR HIRE

WARRIOR PRINCE

VIKING SAGAS

TALES OF ADVENTURE

CHILDREN'S STORIES
ADVENTURES OF TY THE DRAGON
TRAINER
- Ty Catches a Dragon
- Ty and the Bandits
- Ty Rescues Princess Lalea

CEREMONIAL DANCE MASKS
Of MEXICO AND GUATEMALA

Adventures of Ty the Dragon Trainer
Book One

Ty
Catches a Dragon

Don Frederickson

Hiawatha Publishing

Published in Clinton Township, Michigan, by Hiawatha
Publishing

www.dwfrederickson@gmail.com

Publisher's Note: This story is a work of fiction. Names,
characters, places, and incidents are either products of the
author's imagination or used fictitiously . All characters are
fictional and any similarity to people living or dead is purely
coincidental.

Cover Design by Donald W. Frederickson

Page Design by Donald W. Frederickson

ISBN 9781976289514

ADVENTURES OF TY THE DRAGON TRAINER

This trilogy:
Adventures of Ty the Dragon Trainer
is dedicated to my Grandson Ty Fred-
ericson who told me he wants to be a
dragon trainer.

TY CATCHES A DRAGON
The first of three books telling the
story of Ty becoming a dragon trainer
and the adventures he encounters as a
result.

Ty the Dragon Trainer

Ty Catches a Dragon

Long, long ago in a land far away was a magical kingdom by the name of Zedwella. It was a land with tall beautiful mountains that reached up through the clouds, and between them lush fertile valleys where the people lived and farmed the land. Zedwella was a rich kingdom. The people lived well and were very happy, but other nearby kingdoms were jealous of Zedwella's riches. They wanted to take what the people of Zedwella had and sometimes raided villages near the border. To protect the people, the kingdom had an army of dragon riding warriors, led by the king. The war dragons of Zedwella were known to be ferocious in battle when ridden by "Star Warriors", the greatest fighters in the land.

In the high mountain valley in the village of Parkerwella, a young boy, Ty, lived with his father, mother and little brother Zac. More than anything in the world Ty wanted to be a dragon trainer. The great flying Star Warriors who rode the dragons were known by all the people as protectors of the Kingdom but when there were celebrations it was the Dragon Master who was always honored by the king and stood beside him. The Dragon Master was in charge of dragon training. Dragons are large flying reptiles and are dangerous temperamental beasts. Their wild nature never completely leaves them and they are hard to train. A dragon trainer must be a strong dedicated warrior who has a special way with the beasts. It takes a very special skill. Few people possessed it. Ty knew he had the skill. Everyone said he was too young to know, but he knew. He was absolutely sure—and he was going to be a dragon trainer.

Every day after school Ty would do his homework and chores then run through the woods to the great cave where the dragons were kept. When he got there something would always be happening. He loved to watch the trainers working with the animals. Handlers would be in the training field with the dragons while the Dragon Master stood in a tower and watched. From time to time he'd shout something to a trainer or come down and help

Dragons are fiercely independent and don't take easily to learning commands. Sometimes they would play dumb or refuse to move as directed. Other times they might try to bite or step on a trainer. Even seasoned war dragons needed almost constant training to keep them from becoming wild again.

Each day some trainers were teaching the huge scaled beasts to respond to new commands, others were teaching their beasts to throw fire as targets burst into flame, and a few who would soon to be ready to be assigned to a Star Warrior were flying on command and practicing battle maneuvers.

Ty would help wherever he could. At first they considered him a pest; always underfoot, but in time became used to him and let him help with small tasks. In time the trainers accepted him. They called him the crazy kid who wanted to be a dragon trainer.

Lord Alfred the Mighty, a warrior of the first rank and the trainer who rode the dragon Blazing Comet took a liking to Ty and said Ty could help him. Ty was excited, he found a place with the dragon trainers, and was sure they would teach him how to train a dragon.

Ty Couldn't wait to tell everyone. He ran all the way home to tell the good news two his family.

"I'm going to be a dragon trainer, I'm going to be a dragon trainer," he shouted as he came into the house.

"That's nice," said his father, "and when is that going to happen?"

"Now," responded Ty. "Lord Alfred just said I could be his assistant."

"Isn't that dangerous," asked his mother. "I'm not sure I want you to get to close to those animals. You could get hurt."

"I won't get hurt," Ty responded.

"What do you think?" She asked her husband."

"He's over there all the time anyway," he said. "I talked to the stable manager the other day about it, and they all like Ty. They'll look out for him."

"We'll okay," his mother said, but you

have to do all your chores after school before you go there, and your school work too."

Zac, Ty's little brother heard the news. "I want to be a dragon trainer too." he shouted.

"You're too young." Ty answered. "Maybe when you get to be my age you can be one."

As Ty ran out of the house, he called back, "I've got to go tell my friends."

"Be home for dinner," is mother called after him.

"You sure it's going to be all right," she asked her husband? He's getting awfully involved with them. He should be spending more time with his friends."

"I'm sure that its just a phase. Once he gets tired of it, he'll find something else."

Ty approached his new duties with all his energy. The dragon stalls in the cave needed cleaning. Food and water needed to be brought to the dragons. Ty worked hard so that Lord Alfred would be proud of him, but it was fun.

Star Warriors who had a special talent were the Dragon Trainers. They would take a young dragon, and over many seasons work trained it to become a war dragon. It was demanding work. Dragons are hard to train. Their wild nature never completely leaves them.

Along with the trainers were handlers, men who worked at keeping the dragons in good order, feeding and watering them, moving them form place to place when needed, getting them prepared for the trainers and putting the dragons back in the cave in their places when training was over. Ty was Lord Alfred's assistant, but spent a great deal of his time with the handlers. From them he learned how to handle a dragon.

Ogden, was Lord Alfred's chief handler. It was his job to keep Blazing Comet, the lord's war dragon ready for the Lord to use at any time. He taught Ty how to behave around a dragon.

"Never sneek up on a dragon," Ogden

woud tell him. "Always let him know you are coming. If you startle him, he's liable to set you on fire and that would be good."

"Guess not," Ty responded and was careful to follow Ogden's directions.

"And always watch the dragon's tail. If he is angry or irritated he will switch his tail. When that happens, it's best to stay away from him for a while

"When will it stop?" Ty questioned.

"Usually when he gets hungry. He'll put up with you when you bring something to eat. Dragons arn't very smart, byt they are not dumb either."

Ty learned quickly and within the period of the passing of a moon was able to help Ogden with his Blazing Comet.

Lord Alfred was pleased. He noticed that Ty did have a way with Blazing

Ty Catches a Dragon

Comet who accepted him and at times even seemed to indicate that he liked Ty which was unusual for a dragon.

Dragons need a lot of exercise. They need to fly regularly. Much of Lord Alfred's time consisted of training new dragons. So taking the dragon flying was often Ogden's job

One day after school, when Ty arrived at the dragon cave, Ogden was waiting.

"Like to go flying?" he asked. "I'm taking Blazing Comet out for her exercise.

"Me? fly?" Ty excleimed. "Wow."

"Climb on up behind me," Ogden called as he pulled himself up by the climbing rope. "This girl needs to get out and spread her wings."

Ty's first ride was the thrill of a lifetime.

"Hang on tight," Ogden called as he commanded Blazing Comet to take off.

They flew out over the village of Parkerwella, then came back and circled the training field. Ty waived down to Lord Alfred who was working with a young dragon.

Lord Alfred broke into a smile, and waived back.

As they flew away from the village, Ty got a feeling that this was where he belonged and that dragons were to be his destiny. He not only wanted to be a dragon trainer, but one day he would to be a Star Warrior too, just like Lord Alfred.

Ty Catches a Dragon

Feeding time was special. Lord Alfred always fed Blazing Comet himself.

"I always want her to know who her master is," he would say. "Dragons tend to get along best with those who feed them."

When it came to feeding time, Lord Alfred' handler Ogden would come to the dragon's area pushing a large cart full of chunks of meat. Lord Alfred would take a hunk of meat, throw it up in the air and Blazing Comet would catch it.

Ty always came to watch. He was fascinated as the great beast would wait for a hunk of meat to be thrown, grab it in her mighty jaws and swallow it whole. Then Blazing Comet would stretch her long neck bend forward with her head swaying from side to side, looking down on the warrior and growl softly waiting for another piece to be thrown.

After a couple passings of the moon, Lord Alfred gave Ty a piece of meat to throw. "You try," he said. "Blazing Comet likes you. Lets see how she repspsonds."

Ty took a piect of meat pulled his arm back as far as he could and threw it with all his might, as high as he could. Blazing Comet caught and swallowed it in one motion, then bent her head down in front of Ty and looked him in the face and growled softly.

"Yes, she likes you," Lord Alfred said. From now on you can help me feed her."

One day Ty had many chores to do at

home and he came late. When he got to the training field he was out of breath from running through the woods. Lord Alfred was on the training field, sitting on the back of a young dragon, teaching him to throw fire on command. The dragon, almost an adult now, stood between five and six men tall and would soon be assigned to a warrior, and take his place as a war dragon.

"Prepare fire," Lord Alfred called loudly as he tapped the dragon on the neck with his training staff. The dragon reared back on its hind legs and spread its wings out. Then he pointed his staff at a target of an Arvark and yelled, "Fire!" A stream of flame flew through the air from the dragon and the target burst into flame. "Good," he'd call as he rubbed the side of the animal's neck with the staff as a reward; the young dragon emitted a low growl.

As Ty came up to them, Lord Alfred called down. "Let's see how good his aim is. Stand next to that Arvark dummy."

Ty walked over to the straw dummy, stood beside it and tried to look brave. "What if he misses?" Ty called.

"Guess I'll have to find another helper."

Ty used all his courage and stood tall.

"Okay better not miss, then," he called

back as the arvark dummy beside him burst into flame.

"You've got courage kid," the lord called down to him. "I know some warriors that wouldn't have done that."

"It's because you're a good trainer. One day I want to be just as good as you."

Lord Alfred laughed. "Let's go feed Blazing Comet. She's been waiting for you."

A couple of cycles of the moon later, when came to the dragon cave, Ty thought it was just going to be another day of routine training. Blazing Comet stretched its long neck down where her head met his and looked him in the eye. She was waiting for him to scratch her nose. It was a daily ritual. All of the handlers, were amazed at the two of them. No one else wanted to get near that dragon. She was a touchy one.

"Hi Blazing Comet," Ty said as he raked his nails back and forth over her nose. "How's my girl today?" She let out a little guttural growl of pleasure. Dragons, being temperamental, don't seem to like much of anything, but Blazing Comet liked Ty. He had a way with her and the other dragons. They seemed to respond easily to him.

It was time to feed Blazing Comet. Ogden, pulling a cart full of meat, came up to them.

Blazing Comet, stretched her long neck down and smelled the cart, as she did each day, then raised it waiting for Ty, the Lord, or Ogden to throw her a hunk of meat.

After he threw the first hunk, Lord Afred casually said, "We're going dragon hunting in a couple of days."

"I'm coming too, I hope ?" asked Ogden. I love the hunting trips."

"Of course," replied Lord Alfred. "How could I leave my best handler behind."

"How do you catch a dragon?" Ty wanted to know.

"Very carefully," Lord Alfred replied. "They bite."

"They don't burn you up?"

"No," Ogden replied. "We only catch young ones who arn't old enough to spit fire yet."

"Wow," Ty responded, as he looked at Ogden. "You sure are lucky."

"Think so," Lord Alfred asked.

"Sure do" Ty said. "It sounds like a lot of fun."

"Then, maybe you would you like to come along, Lord Alfred said.

"Me? You want me to go dragon hunting with you?"

"Sure. You're a good helper and I think you deserve to come along. We're leaving for Forest Canyon in three days."

Ty couldn't wait until the day for dragon hunting arrived. Each afternoon, after school, when he came to the dragon cave, he had lots of questions for Ogden. He wanted to know everything about dragon hunting.

"How will we catch them?"

"We'll find a colony. When we do, Star

Ty Catches a Dragon

Warriors will fly in on their war dragons and scare the adults off, then we'll catch the young ones who can't fly yet. We're looking for the ones about a year old. They are the ones that can be trained"

"They won't fly away too?"

"They'll be scared. Since they were born they were taught to hide from danger. They'll be hiding. We'll have to find them."

"Then what?"

"We throw a looped rope over there heads and drag them out of their hiding places, or if they run, we chase them and throw the rope over them.

School was going to be out the day they went dragon hunting. Ty could hardly wait.

For the next three days all he could talk about to his family or friends, was dragon hunting. His friends thought he was the luckiest guy in the world. His mother, on the other hand, was worried.

"It must be dangerous," she said with concern.

"We only catch little ones," Ty would reply. Anyway Lord Alfred will be there. He won't let anything happen.

"Still, you have to be careful," she would reply.

Ty's brother Zac thought he was the greatest. He wanted to be just like him.

"Can I come too?" he asked over and over.

"You're to young," Ty always said. "Maybe when you get older."

The day came when caravan of eight wagons, with cages on them, left the village of Parkerwella on a journey through the mountain passes to the country where wild dragons lived. Pulled by giant lizards, the wagons moved slowly, hardly faster than a man could walk. On the third wagon, Ty sat between Lord Alfred and Ogden. He could hardly wait until they got to the canyon. Dragon hunting was going to be fun.

"Are we going to catch a big one?" Ty asked.

"Not too big," Lord Alfred answered. "We need to catch one before he starts breathing fire or he'll burn you up." He looked down at Ty. "Can't have that, can we?"

"Nope, don't think mom would like that."

"No, I think not. We'll find a young one, easy to train."

As the hunting party got closer to the dragon colony, the mood became more serious. The talk between the men stopped. They would be there soon and didn't want the dragons to see or hear them coming.

Late in the morning the caravan came to the mountain range where the dragon colony was. They stopped and the men got out.

"We climb the rest of the way," Lord Alfred said. "Don't want to spook them."

One by one, in a line the group climbed the small mountain peak. Spread out through the high mountains of Zedwella there were a large number of plateaus, flat areas at different levels; areas that looked like parts of the mountain tops were shaved off. A large number of the kingdon's people lived on these plateus and had prosperous farms on them.

Ty Catches a Dragon

The dragon colony they were after was on a high mountain plateau of one of the smaller mountains in the wilderness area. Other large mountains ringed it.

"We've got to be really quiet now," Lord Alfred said as they reached the summit.

They hid behind some bolders and peered over the top. Out in front of them was a colony of dragons in an alcove wth caves Inside the caves would be their nests.

The lord pointed to a mountain peak in the distance   "See that? That's one of their dragons watching over the colony. If he sees us he will raise the alarm."

"Then what," Ty asked.

"Lots of trouble for us," Lord Alfred responded. "He'll alert the others and the big ones will come after us."

"That doesn't sound good." Ty said.

"Not at all," responded Ogden.

"See that," Lord Alfred said to Ty as he turned and pointed to a mountain top in the distance behind them.

"I don't see anything," Ty followed.

Ty Catches a Dragon

"At that peak is one of our war dragons." Lord Alfred pointed to a distant mountain. Looking closely Ty could see a dragon sitting near the summit.

"In the distance, he looks just like a wild one, but behind him, out of sight, are the Zedwalla war dragons. If we get spotted, they will be here in time to help us."

"So we're not in any danger," Ty responded as he remembered his mother's concern.

"There's always some danger," Ogden said. "You must be very careful around dragons, especially wild ones."

We've got to be quiet from here," Lord Alfred said. "The dragon colony is just over that rise.

The little hunting party watching the dragon colony waied for Lord Alfred's Instructions. It was a large colony with more than forty dragons nesting together in a group of caves. Ty watched and listened as the hunters made thier final plans.

Turning back to the dragon colony, Lord Alfred said, "I see a couple of nice ones," See that silver one?" He pointed toward a dragon on the edge of the group. "I want to catch him."

"Looks like a good one to me," Ty observed. "Kinda big for training though isn't he?"

Ty Catches a Dragon

"I like them big," Lord Alfred said. "All the warriors want the dragons I train."

"We're about ready," the lord said to the other members of the group.

He looked to Ty and said, "When we get down there, be careful and stay out of the way. I don't want you to get hurt."

The party of hunters broke into two groups and quietly approached the dragon colony from two sides. At the right moment, the Dragon Master sounded a horn and the warriors stood up and beat metal drums which made an awfully loud noise. Suddenly, there was total chaos. Dragons were running and flying in every direction. The dragons that were on the cliffs watching immediately charged the hunting party. In the group the big male dragons formed a defense against the drummers.

At the same time, the attacking war dragons of Zedwella flew in and met the attacking colony dragons. They engaged in an air battle which the Zedwella dragons won. The colony dragons flew away to distant mountain peeks always keeping the Zedwella dragaons in sight.

The next stage was for the war dragons to take on the colony's defence dragons, It was a short battle. Zedwella's war dragons drove the wild ones off. They flew to nearby mountain cliffs and also watched the invasion of their colony. As the big adult dragons flew away the smaller ones ran and hid.

The Star Warriors sat on their war dragons, in the middle of the colony, to keep the big adults from coming back while the hunters started looking for the dragons that were hiding.

Ty Catches a Dragon

Young dragons, not yet adults, about three to four times the height of a man were found and lassoed. Once a rope was thrown around a young dragon's neck, the hunters would drag a resisting animal back to the open area to await the arrival of the wagons with cages.

"Over there." Lord Alfred shouted as

a young dragon jumped out of hiding and ran. He pointed for Ty to run alongside, as he ran after the fleeing dragon. "Head him off."

Ty ran beside the animal, waving his arms above his head to keep it from turning off. Lord Alfred threw the loop around its neck and pulled hard. Ty grabbed the rope behind Lord Alfred and pulled with all his strength. The strong young animal dragged the two of them along behind as it strove to get away.

"Don't stop pulling; we've got to hold him," Lord Alfred commanded as Ty strained with all his might and dug his heels into the ground. The young dragon continued to pull them skidding across the ground. Slowly, the dragon started to tire.

"Keep pulling. We're winning," Alfred shouted and Ty pulled harder.

Ty Catches a Dragon

Suddenly, the dragon stopped, turned, raised up on its hind legs and glared at them.

"Lookout, they bite," Lord Alfred yelled as he dove off to the side. The dragon's head lunged for Ty. Ty dodged to the side as its teeth missed by inches.

"We need to get another lasso on it!" Lord Alfred called

Ty grabbed a rope, threw a loop over the young dragon's head and pulled from the opposite side. The beast shook and fought, but continued to tire until it finally stopped fighting. When subdued, they led it back and put it in the wagon.

"Looks like I've got my next dragon to work with," Lord Alfred said. "We get the ones we catch for our next animal to train."

"He's beautiful," Ty exclaimed, as he

admired the dragon; a pale gray beast about the height of four men, covered with large rough gray scales, a long neck, full body with large hind legs and a long tail.

While the men were securing their captured dragons and preparing for the trip home, Ty decided to go explorering and wandered into a dragon cave to look around. As he heard Lord Alfred's voice calling, "Time to come back," he noticed movement against a far wall, in a hollowed out space. He went over to look.

He peered in and as his eyes adjusted to the light, he saw a large pair of eyes looking back at him—an infant dragon that was only a few weeks old.

"Aren't you a nice fellow," Ty said to the young dragon that stood taller than him. He searched around and found a rope. Looping it, he slowly approached the infant dragon. It was shaking, its eyes filled with terror.

"Easy boy," Ty said softly.

The young animal growled sharply while moving back and forth in its hiding place looking for a way to get past him. There was no escape.

Ty came closer, holding up the rope loop to throw over the young animal's head. Suddenly it bared its teeth and struck at Ty to bite him. Ty sidestepped, dropped the loop over the animal's neck, and quickly took up the slack. Then he pulled the young dragon out into the room.

Suddenly, the animal turned to run, pulling Ty behind him. Ty braced his feet and pulled back against the dragon. The dragon pulled hard with him skidding across the floor behind it. Ty pulled back hard and for a second felt a little slack in the rope. He desperately slung the rope around one of the rocks on the floor to secure it.

The young dragon pulled against his bounds and in spurts pulled the rock along behind until it became too weak to continue. In terror, the dragon turned and tried to bite Ty again. He moved out or of range and let the dragon pull and fight the rope until it was tired out.

Talking softly to calm the dragon, Ty approached and stroked the side of its head. The creature stood motionless letting Ty touch him, but as soon as Ty pulled on the rope again, the dragon continued fighting it. Ty had to work hard to wrestle the dragon but was able to bring it back to where Lord Alfred waited.

He stood with the dragon behind him as he worked to catch his breath.

Ty Catches a Dragon

"I got me one too," he said. He could hardly hold back the big grin that wanted to come across his face.

"Look here," Alfred called to other hunters. "The kid's caught a dragon too."

"You really should leave it here," the Dragon Master, who was seated on top of his dragon, said as he looked down on Ty and the young dragon. "He's too young to train and he'd be a lot of work to take care of until he is old enough."

"I promise I'll do the extra work and take good care of him," Ty pleaded, "and when he gets older, Lord Alfred can train him as a war dragon."

"The kids a good helper," Lord Alfred said. "He'll be good on his promise and take care of the young animal."

As they waited for the wagons, Lord

Alfred directed Ty to look around at the surrounding mountain tops. It seemed that dragons were everywhere looking down watching the men who had captured their young ones.

"A dragon, sitting on a mountain top is a dangerous thing," he told Ty. You never know what they are going to do. Sometimes they will just watch and at other times they will attack. If we didn't have the war dragons with us, they would cause a lot of trouble for us."

Late that morning, the wagons arrived where the captured dragons were held.

"We really should leave him here," the Dragon Master said again as he too came over and looked at Ty's dragon. He's young.

"It might be a good experiment," Lord

Ty Catches a Dragon

Alfred mused. He liked Ty and it intrigued him to see how the boy would approach the task of caring for the young animal. He had spunk, and he was good with the war dragons. "And it might be good for Ty. He's a good helper. I think he deserves a try with the beast."

The Dragon Master, thought for a long time, then he and Lord Alfred went for a walk to discuss it privately. When they came back, he said the Ty could bring the young dragon back, but if it didn't work out, he'd have to let him go back to the wild.

As they rode back to the village of Parkerwella, Ty's young dragon came with them. Ty couldn't stop grinning. He couldn't believe he really caught a dragon.

"What are you going to name him?" Lord Alfred asked.

"Me, name him?"

"Yes, you caught him, so you've got to give him a name."

Ty thought for a moment. "I'll name him Morning Star since he is a new born dragon."

"Good name," Lord Alfred replied. "And you're going to take care of him; feed him, clean his corral,"

"You bet," Ty answered. "Every day, I'll make sure he has whatever he needs."

"You know," Lord Alfred said, "being so young, what he really needs is a companion, more than just someone looking after him. It's going to take a lot more of your time."

"I can do that," Ty said as he thought to himself, 'Wow, a dragon of my own, just like the trainers and warriors have…

Ty Catches a Dragon

Morning Star was still an infant dragon, only starting to develop the features found on an adult. He had a large grey body with a bulging stomach, a short thick neck and stubby legs. He had small scales all over his body, not overlapping yet; they were soft only starting to grow.

"Ain't very pretty," Lord Alfred said as Ty came into the cave the next day. The young dragon was corralled in a holding pen where he could walk around. "he's been crying all night, and won't eat this morning."

"That's bad isn't it," Ty replied.

"Not good," followed Ogden who just came up to where they were talking. "We gotta do something or he won't last. Maybe he isn't ready to eat meat yet. Maybe he's still on mother's milk. Perhaps we could hook up something for him to drink from like he gets from his mother."

"What do you think would work," asked Ty

"How about a bucket with a hole in the bottom and a plug in it until it,s ready to be used." said Ogden.

"Great Idea. I'll make one," Ty said.

Ty's father donated a bucket and made a hole in. Ty took it back to the cave with the dragons. Ogden found a couple of pails full of milk.

"Ready," He asked, after they filled Ty's bucket.

"Ready," replied Ty.

They entered the corral with the dragon. The young animal was terrified. It wouldn't let them get near and kept dodging around them when they tried.

"Not going to work," Lord Alfred said as he came over to watch them. He called to the handlers in the area "Someone find some ropes we're going to need some help."

It took five men to hold the young animal down. They placed two ropes around it's neck, one to each side, and one around each back foot, then moved him against the corral fence. Ty climbed on top the fence. The struggling animal as it tried to get away and tried to bite him twice. Ty strained to hold the bucket above its head.

"Hold steady there, boy," Ty called as he pulled the plug from the bottom of the bucket and lifted it over the dragon's head.

Milk poured from the bottom into the young animal's mouth. Morning Star immediately drank it, then put his mouth around the bucket and started to suck the milk out.

"Good," said Lord Alfred approvingly. "He's drinking it, so it looks like we have a solution."

Ty Catches a Dragon

They had to fill the bucket three more times before the young animal stopped drinking.

"Guess we're going to do that every day." Lord Alfred said; "actually twice a day, I think.

"I'll get up before school," Ty replied and feed him then and again after school."

The next afternoon when Ty came in to feed Morning Star, the Dragon Master and Lord Alfred were waiting for him.

"He's been crying all last night and all day today," the Dragon Master said. "He's not ready to be away from his mother. We should return him back to the wild."

"I know that hurts, but I don't know what else to do," Lord Alfred followed.

As they were talking, the handlers were bringing one of the dragons, a female who had been there a few changes of the seasons, back into the cave. As it passed Morning Star's corral, the young animal made a heck of a loud racket, sounding like it was screaming. He pulled and strained at the ropes holding him. Trying to get to the other dragon. The female dragon stopped, looked at Morning Star and made low growling sounds.

Morning Star broke free of the ropes and charged the corral fence, crashing through it. He ran up to the female dragon then huddled next to it. The female bent its' head down and nuzzled him as it continued to make low soothing sounds.

Ty Catches a Dragon

"Well look at that," Lord Alfred said. "Isn't that amazing."

"Is that his mother?" Ty asked.

"No, to young," the Dragon Master followed, "but it is a female we just brought from the last hunt. We're just starting to train her. "

As they moved toward Morning Star, the new dragon swung its head around toward them, growled loudly and tried to bite the Dragon Master.

"Kind of protective, wouldn't you say," Lord Alfred stated as he jumped back.

"Looks that way," the Dragon Master replied.

"Is that good?" questioned Ty. "He's quiet now."

"Maybe it will stop those wailing noises

he's been making. Let's see what happens. We'll watch him for a while," the Dragon Master replied.

The handlers, moved the new dragon to its corral and Morning Star followed, all the while staying close to it.

As Ty, Lord Alfred and the Dragon master watched, Morning Star stood close beside the larger dragon. The female dragon stretched its head down and stroked him. Morning Star made some soft cooing sounds, then nuzzled against the larger animal's leg.

Ty got out the bucket, filled it with milk for Morning Star's meal. As he approached, the new dragon drew back its head and growled. It wasn't going to let anyone get close the younger one.

"Best hold off for now," Lord Alfred

said.

"But he'll be hungry," Ty cried.

"Let them be for a while," said the Dragon Master. "Tomorrow will find a way to separate them for a little, and then you will be able to feed him."

Each day the handlers would take the new dragon out leaving Morning Star alone in the corral. Then they would rope the young animal and Ty would feed him. It took a turn of the moon for the young dragon to accept him and come for his milk. By then, the older dragon seemed to know Ty wasn't a threat and accepted him coming near.

It was two more turns of the moon before Ty was able to do anything more with Morning Star. He wouldn't leave the other dragon's side but was used to Ty feeding him.

"How about taking your dragon for a walk," Ogden said one day when Ty arrived the dragon's cave.

"Think he's ready," Ty replied as he looke approvingly at the dragon.

"We'll find out, won't we?" Ogden said.

They put a rope around Morning Star's neck and led him from the cave.

he didn't like Ogden, but followed Ty.

Ty Catches a Dragon

"Just around the outside edges o the field," Lord Alfred instructed as he saw them come out.

Ty led and Morning Star followed behind. He seemed to take to the lead. Ogden followed behind to make sure all went well.   They made two circuts around the outside of the field and Ogden stopped to talk to another handler. Ty and Morning Star continued on alone.

About half way around the field, Ty pulled Morning Star up to walk beside him. The young dragon spooked, jumped off to the side and pulled the rope from Ty's hand; then ran. It cut across the training field running.

"Ty ran as fast as he could to try to catch him, as he yelled, "stop, stop"

All of the dragon trainers, working with

their animals looked up and laughed.

"Go get him," someone called.

"Don't let him get away," another shouted.

"Who's walking who" came through too.

Even young dragons run very fast and Ty was falling behind. Just after it got past the edge of the village, Lord Alfred, riding Blazing Comet landed in front of it and shot a stream of flame in Morning Star's direction. The young dragon stopped in its tracks and stood quivering.

Ty ran up and picked up the rope.

"Hang on tighter," Lord Alfred said then commanded his beast to rise in the air and fly back to the field.

"Morning Star seemed to walk behind

him okay, so he brought Morning Star back to the training field that way.

Each day Ty would take Morning Star for a walk. They always went around the outside edge of the training field. It took a month to get the dragon to walk beside him. The young dragon grew fast and in a matter of two cycles of the moon was twice as tall as Ty. As he became bigger and stronger, his walking became faster. Ty had to trot beside Morning Star now. Soon Ty found he had to run to keep up.

Every day after school, Ty would run to the cave. He always brought something for a snack. Morning star loved chicken feet. It appeared that the young dragon was happy to see Ty and looked forward to his daily training. He seemed attentive to Ty and even responded to his basic commands of "walk by me, stop, run" As dragons go, he was learning.

"He's coming along fine," Lord Alfred said one afternoon when Ty arrived. I think it is now time to start to do some training, make him a Zedwella dragon."

"Wow," Ty responded. "Where do we start?"

"He's been learning how to follow you around the field and responding to basic commands, but it's time to do more. Commands like go right, go left, go forward, go faster, go slower, lay down, stand up are in order now.

Ty Catches a Dragon

Morning Star liked hunks of raw meat which were used in training as rewards for following commands.

"Go left," Ty would call and throw a hunk of meat in that direction. The dragon would quickly turn in the desired direction and gobble up the meat.

"Go right," Ty would call and throw another hunk of meat. Morning Star turned and gobbled it up.

It was not long before the meat ran out. "Go left," Ty called. Morning Star didn't move. "Go left" he called again. Morning star turned and looked at Ty, then stretched his long neck down where his head could sniff the empty bag where the meat was

"Problems," Lord Alfred asked, as he came up to them.

"He won't listen unless I throw meat," Ty responded.

"Guess you will have to get more meat," Lord Alfred said. "In time, he will learn his commands. It just takes time."

It took another two turns of the moon for Ty to teach Morning star just his basic commands; forward, stop, right, left, sit, stand and such.

"He's growing quickly," Lord Alfred said one day. "He's going to be a big one. You're a lucky boy. He'll be a fine war dragon one day."

"I hope so," Ty said. "He isn't too smart though. It is taking forever for him to learn to respond. "He's good as long as I'm giving him rewards, but after they run out, sometimes he listens and sometimes he doesn't"

"He does have a mind of his own," Lord Alfred said. "Some dragons are a little harder to train. He'll come around. Just stick with it."

"I hope so," Ty said. He was proud that Lord Alfred thought he was doing such a good job.

Lord Alfred watched Ty lead the dragon

away and continue his lesson for the day as the Dragon Master walked up and, following his gaze, looked in the same direction.

"Quite the young fellow, don't you think," he said.

"Yes," the lord said. "I wasn't sure he'd stick with it, but he's not only hanging in there he's doing a good job."

"Thats not an easy dragon to train." observed the Dragon Master. "It looks like it's fighting him every inch of the way."

Lord Alfred laughed. "He's up to the challenge, I think. I have to give him that."

"Is he taking up too muh of your time." asked the Dragon Master.

"No, Ogden is helping him. The two of them get along rather well. He's even been taking Ty flying, so when we get to that stage, he'll be ready."

"Think he can handle riding him? That's always the hard stage with a new animal. Even an experienced handler would have his hands full with this one."

"He's game enough," Lord Alfred replied. I hope he's strong enough."

"I hope he doesn't get hurt." the Dragon Master replied. "We really don't have any business letting a boy get on top of one of these wild beasts. Maybe Ogden should break the animal in, or at least take the edge off"

"Problem is," said the lord. "Morning Star won't let him get anywhere near, or any other handler for that matter."

"Best you watch this part closely. If the dragon gets too rough, get him off of it."

**

In the afternoon a couple of days later, Lord Alfred and the Dragon Master, approached Ty when he was on the training field working wth Morning Star.

"Looks like it's time to start riding him," the Dragon Master said when they came up to him. "I think perhaps it's time to ride Morning Star as he goes around the field and learns to follow your commands while you are on him."

"Wow," Ty responded. He looked up at Morning Star and said. "We get to go for a ride. You'll love it."

Lord Alfred said nothing. He smiled. Ty was a brave lad. He knew how dangerous this part of the training was and he didn't flinch. Wild dragons didn't like it when someone first got on their backs.

Ty Catches a Dragon

In their world if something got on top of them, it would be an enemy, another dragon or something tryng to hurt them. It was a natural reaction. They would fight as hard as they could to get whatever was on them off. The same thing happened when a rider got on.

Ty could be hurt. The dragon would try to get him off its back. It didn't happen often but sometimes dragons would step on the fallen rider. He looked at Ty's enthusiasm. He would be crushed if they stopped him now.

Lord Alfred looked seriously at the Dragon Master and said, "I can't tell him no. He's worked too hard. He's earned it."

The Dragon Master called assistants to put a riding harass on the dragon to prepare him for riding. Morning Star didn't like the handlers but Ty held him steady and talked softly to comfort him.

"He's ready," the Dragon Master declared; "Time to climb up and see how well your dragon responds."

Lord Alfred and three handlers held the dragon steady as Ty took the climbing rope with foot loops and climbed up on Morning Star's back. He grasped the harness in one hand and held the other up, signifying he was ready and Lord Alfred let the dragon loose.

Morning Star didn't like Ty on his back at all. He immediately jumped in the air to try to throw him off. He jumped up and down a number of times and twisted sideways as he jumped. Ty lost his grip was thrown into the air and hit the ground hard.

"Lord Alfred ran up. "Are you hurt? He

asked.

"No," Ty got up and rubbed his arm. He had an angry grimace on his face as he looked up at the young dragon. who was standing there defiantly watching them.

"You have to let him know who's boss," Lord Alfred said. "Morning Star is going to be a hard one to train. His wild side will never leave him and he's going to fight you all the way. He's big for his age and he has a strong spirit."

"You're going to have to teach him that you are in charge not him. This is the hardest stage of dragon training and It's going to take a lot of work, but I think you will tame him."

"We're not done," Ty looked the dragon straight in the eyes and said sharply "Hold him down," Ty commanded the handlers.

He grabbed the climbing rope, pulled it tight, pulled himself up, set down on the dragon's back, grabbed the harness and hollered down, "Let him loose." Morning Star, started jumping and twisting again. Ty held on to the harness with all his strength.

Ty became unseated but didn't let go of the harness. He held on, bumping up and down, as his legs flapped behind him.

"Let go," Lord Alfred shouted. "Let go."

Again Ty hit the ground hard. This time he got up and was limping.

"Enough for today," Lord Alfred advised.

He turned to Ogden and said, "Take him back to the cave and let him rest now."

Turning back to Ty, he laughed, then

broke into a big smile and said, "This ones a fighter for sure, one of the wildest I have seen in a long time, but keep it up and I think you will win. In time he will get used to you and will calm down.

Ty's face broke into a broad smile, proud that the lord thought he did well,

"But," Lord Alfred continued. "best be prepare, it may take quite some time."

Every day, Ty came to the cave and the handlers harnessed Morning Star and Ty climbed on his back to try to ride him. After a number of days, the young dragon started to accept him, but he wasn't happy.

When Ty would first get on his back, he'd buck a few times, and settle down a little but never completely. It was obvious he didn't like someone on him. It took a turn of the moon before Morning Star really accepted him and he was able just to have the dragon walk around the outside of the training field.

.

The day came when Lord Alfred met Ty when he arrived and said, "Ok, it's time to teach him to follow your commands while you're riding him.

Ogden helped Ty get the dragon harnesses up.

"It's about time," Ty confided in him. "Now we can get to work."

"It may be harder than you think," Ogden said. Remember, he doesn't like following commands."

"He learned them before, he can learn them again. Ty stated sharply. "Anyway he does good when we are on the ground together."

They led the dragon out of the cave onto the field, where Lord Alfred and the Dragon Master were waiting.

"Climb up and lets go," Lord Alfred said as he held the climbing rope out for Ty.

Ty climbed up and held the riding harness tightly, Three handlers held the dragon steady "Easy boy," Ty called. "Easy now. It's only me."

"OK, now use your commands," Lord Alfred shouted from the ground. "Get him to follow them and he will calm down."

"Stand still," Ty commanded and Morning Star stopped jumping and bucking.

"Good "said Ty "Now go forward." Morning Star started to walk.

"Go right," and Morning Star turned left.

"Stop," Ty commanded and the dragon continued to walk past the Dragon Master.

"He's not doing very well," Ty called down to the men on the ground "He's not following my commands."

"Keep trying. You're doing good." the Dragon Master called back up to him. "Now it's practice, practice and more practice."

Suddenly Morning Star started to buck again and spun in circles.

"Hold boy," Ty called, and Morning Star bucked harder.

"He's a feisty one," the Dragon Master

called up to him. "Hold on"

"Stop," Ty yelled again and again.

Finally Morning Star tired, came to a stop and stood motionless in the middle of the training field.

"You've got your work cut out for you." Lord Alfred called up to him. "This is what being a dragon trainer is all about. You have to teach him who is boss."

"And remember," the Dragon Master called up to him. "You have to know how to ride without falling off." He laughed loudly, "especialy when you start to fly with him. So this is good practice for that too."

"Yes," it's better to fall off now on the ground instead of later up in the clouds," Lord Alfred added. He laughed, "It hurt less."

Every day Ty came to the Dragon cave and tried to ride Morning Star. The young dragon reluctantly followed his commands but with a lot of resistance. He wasn't responding well and bucked a lot. Ty had to hang on tightly to keep from falling off.

One day, Lord Alfred came out on the training field riding Blazing Comet, walked up and Commanded "Fire" and the dragon shot a burst of flame out in front of Morning Star who immediately stopped in his tracks. Blazing Star was three times the size of the young dragon.

"In the wild," Lord Alfred called down, "young dragons learn by imitating the older ones."

"Tell him to walk," Lord Alfred called.

"Walk," Ty yelled. Morning star stood still, "Walk," Ty commanded again. Sill Morning Star didn't move.

Lord Alfred came up behind them with Blazing Comet, "Shoot fire," he commanded. The dragon shot a stream of fire singeing Morning Star's tail.

The dragon jumped ahead and started to walk.

"Tell him to turn left," Lord Alfred called.

The young dragon turned slightly toward the left.

Another stream of fire shot out next to Morning Star, who turned all the way to the left to get away from it.

For the rest of the day and for two more days, Lord Alfred and Blazing Comet helped Morning Star to learn that commands must be followed. Ty continued to work with him and the young dragon learned to respond to his directions quickly. Soon Ty was able to direct the Morning Star where ever he wanted him to go.

Ty Catches a Dragon

One day Ty came to the cave, and Morning Star greeted him with a puff of smoke blown from his nose.

"Oh, Oh," Lord Alfred said as he saw the greeting. He called the Dragon Master over. "It's time," he said pointing to the dragon's head, a whiff of smoke curling from its nose.

"Time for what?" Ty asked.

"He's starting to breathe fire. This is a dangerous time. Once he learns to shoot fire, he might burn up anything he doesn't like."

"He doesn't like me," a nearby handler said.

"Best not get to close then," Lord Alfred said.

"It's time to train him to shoot fire," the Dragon Master said. "Harness him up and come out to the training field."

A short time later, Ty and Morning Star came out to the field and stopped at a spot the dragon Master pointed to next to another dragon. In front of them were three large Arvark dummies.

"Command him," blow fire" the dragon master called.

"Shoot fire," Ty yelled. The dragon next to Morning Star sent a stream of flame out and one of the dummies burst into flame.

"Command him again," the Dragon Master called.

"Shoot fire," Ty yelled. The same thing happened.

Ty Catches a Dragon

On the fifth time, a small flame came from Morning Star.

"He did it," Ty called down. "He threw fire,"

"Yes," the dragon master called back. Now you have to teach him to aim at a target."

Ty carried a pouch of meat with him.

"Shoot fire," Ty shouted as he used his lead and turned the dragon's head in the direction he wanted the flame to go. For a reward, he threw a hunk of meat out in front of the dragon, who would snap it up before it hit the ground.

Day after day they practiced until Morning Star shot flames and hit target after target without error.

"He's doing good," Lord Alfred said at the end of the day when they returned to the cave. "Tomorrow you will teach him to throw fire at targets when you are on the ground next to him. He needs to know how to protect you in all instances. "But, he's a wild one," Lord Alfred said while looking at the dragon with a knowing eye. "It's a dangerous time. Once he gets to know he can shoot fire at will, he's likely to go after anything he wants to."

A couple of days later, Ty came to the cave to work the dragon. He wasn't in the place he normally frequented. He quickly found Lord Alfred.

"Where is Morning Star? he asked. He's not in the cave."

"We had to move him" Lord Alfred said. "He was shooting fire at the handlers."

"Mick and Armin, I'll bet," Ty followed. "He doesn't like them much."

"Yes, and he shot one at me." Lord Alfred growled, "and burnt my arm." He tenderly held his arm that was bandaged.

"That's not good, is it?" Ty said.

"Darn right, it's not." Lord Alfred was angry. "If he wants to be a war dragon of Zedwella, he's going to have to learn to control himself or I'll have Blazing Comet take care of him, and that will be the last of him.

"Right now we're keeping him away from everyone; no telling where he will throw fire. You're going to have to teach him when and were to direct it."

"But," Ty exclaimed. "How can I do that?"

"The training staff, my boy," Lord Alfred said as he handed Ty a wooden pole that was taller than he was. "You have to learn to ride now with one hand holding the harness handle and the other holding the staff. You will need this skill when you are flying your dragon."

"When will that be," Ty answered excitedly. He couldn't wait.

"First, you'll have to get him to throw fire only when you direct it. Ride him on the field and when he throws fire you haven't commanded, and he will, rap him on the neck, near his head, with the staff. You won't hurt him, but he won't like it. Do this every day and maybe in the course of one turn of the moon, he will follow your direction."

Every day Ty and Morning Star practiced. True to Lord Alfred's prediction, it took a full turn of the moon before Morning Star became trained enough to be trusted to bring back in the dragon cave with other dragons

.

Morning Star continued to grow quickly. The day arrived when he was three times the height of Ty and was starting to develop the characteristics of an adult dragon.

His scales had grown and were now over-lapping, shielding his body. His legs were short, but thick and strong. His neck grew long, like an adult, and was more flexible. His wings were almost developed, large and strong .

Ty could hardly wait. Morning Star was almost the size of a full sized dragon now and still growing. He was getting stronger each day and would soon be flying.

Recently, Morning Star was jumping and flapping his wings and coming off the ground for a few feet and sailing for short distances across the training field. Every few days he was able to fly further.

It was tme for him to learn to fly on command.

Lord Alfred set up a new harness for the young dragon. It attached snuggly to his body and had a very long lead. It was the same as they used to train all new dragons to fly on command. One end of the lead was attached to the dragon, the other to to a large rock or small boulder, which pulled against the animal if it wanted to go too high or too far. Four to six handlers would manage the rope letting slack in it teaching the dragon to "fly" on command shouted from the ground and then pulling him down to "land" again on command.

Morning Star's lead was twice as long as they normally used. He needed greater distance to effectively train his musels that would be use in flying free. Ty and three handlers managed the rope. Morning Star loved it. He'd fly up, come down and fly up again. It was just like play to him. Soon he was sailing high above them as the handlers on the ground ran to keep up.

Ty awakened early. The sun was just starting to peak over the horizon. He had not slept much during the night and could hardly wait. Today he was going to learn to fly a dragon. The day before, the Dragon Master who was in charge of the training and care of the dragons of Zedwella, the ferocious beasts ridden by the Dragon Warriors, had told him it was time to learn.

As he came to the training field, Ty was thrilled. He could hardly believe that he was going to learn to fly a dragon. He had flown with Ogden a number of times but only once with Lord Alfred who took him for a short ride. Now was different, now he was going to learn to command the dragon in the air, then he would teach Morning Star.

It was ten passing of the moon cycles since Ty captured the young dragon and he worked hard teaching it to follow his commands. The dragon had grown quickly and was becoming stronger every day. The Dragon Master said it was big enough to be able to fly now and it's dragon trainer, Ty, would soon have to train it to follow commands while in the air for it to be considered a war dragon of Zedwella.

"He's a big one; ," the dragon master observed as he admired Morning Star," and greeted Ty, "Yes it's time for you to learn to fly. Do you think you're ready?

Ty grinned and his eyes lit up. "Sure am," he said.

"Then, let's get started," Lord Alfred said.

They walked over to the area where Blazing Comet stayed. "You'll learn on Blazing Comet then when you've learned you can ride Morning Star."

"Great," Ty replied, a beaming smile crossed his face.

"Climb up on his back," Lord Alfred said as he held the lead to his dragon. The beast was in a resting position on his stomach.

The large silver dragon, whose neck was turned, and head tilted was staring down at him. Little puffs of smoke drifted from its nose.

Ty grabbed the climbing rope, put one foot in a loop and pulled himself hand over hand up the side of the dragon, using the loops in the rope for steps, then positioned himself on its bare back and took hold of the hand strap and held it tight.

Lord Alfred climbed up and sat behind Ty.

"I'm in front," Ty exclaimed. "I thought I'd be holding on to you and watching while you told me how to do it."

"You're doing the flying today. That's how you learn."

"Comet up," Lord Alfred shouted, and the dragon rose to its feet and stood tall waiting for another command.

Lord Alfred commanded the dragon to walk to the cave entrance.

"Lets try a couple of simple commands first." Lord Alfred told Ty. "Tell him to raise up."

"Raise up," shouted Ty and the dragon rose on its hind feet, with its wings spread.

"Now say 'fire'," Lord Alfred whispered in Ty's ear.

Ty Catches a Dragon

"Fire," Ty shouted and the dragon blew a flame reaching a distance of thirty feet.

"Wow,"

"That's how you tell everyone to watch out, don't mess with me, that you are a mighty warrior and dangerous." Lord Alfred said with a laugh.

"And I'm a mighty warrior?" Ty asked.

"Someday, Ty. Some day you and your dragon Morning Star will be a warrior team, and people will know and respect you. But now you are learning to be a trainer. The rest will come later."

Lord Alfred gave Ty the command staff used to direct the dragon. The beast would respond to both voice commands and being struck sharply by the staff directing it to rise up or fly down and turn from side to side.

Today we learn voice commands," Lord Alfred said; staff commands comes later.

"Tell him to fly forward."

"fly Forward," Ty yelled and the dragon took a few quick steps flapped its wings and rose off the ground.

"Go Up," whispered the lord.

"Go up," Ty yelled and the dragon rose higher.

For the next hour, Lord Alfred gave Ty directions and they practiced giving commands and the dragon responded to Ty, as directed.

The sun was close to setting. They were flying out over the mountains, and Lord Alfred shouted to Ty, "Take us home."

"What do I say," Ty. He looked around, just mountains. "Which way do I go?"

Ty Catches a Dragon

"You know what to do. Use what you learned today and figure it out. You can do it."

Ty looked out over the mountains. He couldn't see Parkerwella from where they were. Which way did he have to go to get them back? He thought about it then realized that the sun would set in the west. They had gone toward the afternoon sun when they left, so they must go away from the sun to get home. With his decision, Ty gave commands to the dragon. Blazing Comet responded as directed and flew back to the training field.

When they landed and got down on the ground again, Lord Alfred told Ty he had done a wonderful job with his first lesson and they would start to work with Morning Star to teach him to obey the commands just like Blazing Comet did.

Morning Star loved to fly and learned quickly. Soon Ty was flying the young animal by himself. The dragon responded easily to his commands. Each day they would fly over the training field and out over the village of Parkerwella practicing the maneuvers Lord Alfred gave them. Ty could see his house and school as they flew over and waived to his brother Zac. Zac wanted to be a dragon trainer too, just like his brother. Ty promised Zac that when he was a little older, he would take him for rides on Morning Star.

One day the Dragon Master was waiting at the cave when Ty finished giving Morning Star his flying exercise.

Ty Catches a Dragon

"He's coming along wonderfully," the Dragon Master said as Ty climbed down, "and you are becoming a good trainer. Your dragon will become a great war dragon one day."

Ty stood, a big grin on his face, not knowing what to say. A complement like that from the Dragon Master was special. He didn't hand many out to his trainers.

The Dragon Master continued, "Morning Star is growing fast and getting larger. He needs more exercise to develop his strength. It's time you fly out over the mountains and through the valleys, and letting him fly as hard and fast as he can.

"I can do that," Ty asked.

"Yes, you can handle it, my boy," the Dragon Trainer responded. "I've watched you. You were born to fly a dragon. Make him a strong animal and a fast flyer. He will need to be very, very, strong to become a war dragon of Zedwella.

Ty thought he was the luckiest boy in the world. Every afternoon, Ty and Morning Star would fly out over the mountains, until the sun started to set. Morning Star loved to fly and Ty loved riding him.

He flew Moring Star to the school to show the dragon to all of his friends. He even took his brother Zac for a ride.

He thought it couldn't get any better.

Ty Catches a Dragon

Not long after, Ty came to the dragon cave. Morning Star was not in his area wth the female dragon he had been staying close to.

As he looked around, Ty asked Ogden, "Where's my boy today,"

"Ogden hesitated, then said, "He escaped--he's gone."

"Escaped," gasp Ty. "How?"

"The female dragon he was staying close too got loose and flew off. Morning Star followed her."

"Wasn't he secure?" Ty asked.

"He was on a rope tie down," Ogden answered. He's a smart dragon. It only took a burst of fire and up the rope went in smoke. Then he took off after the other dragon.

Lord Alfred came up to them. "I'm sorry. Sometime this happens. The dragons are still wild animals, you know."

"We have to do something," Ty cried.

"We'll get him back," Lord Alfred promised. "I have a lot of time and work invested in trining both of the dragons. I'm not about to have to do it again with new beasts."

He looked at Ty and Ogden. "We three will find them and capture them again. They have to be somewhere about, probably hooked up with another dragon colony. Tomorrow we will start looking."

Ty Catches a Dragon

Lord Alfred left, and Ogden confided to Ty, "Let's hope we can get him back soon. It's going to have to be fast though. When they find a wild group it's like they never had the training. They revert to being wild almost immediately.

Ty was despondent. All that he could think of was that Morning Star was gone. Would he ever get him back? Lord Alfred said they would, but he was worried. He heard the other handlers talking, saying that it was the last that they would see of "those" dragons.

"Good riddance," said the handler that Morning Star shot fire at from time to time. He never really hurt the handler, but let him know he wasn't liked.

All of the handlers were careful around Morning Star. He was starting to approach adult hood and was becoming more agressive. Dragons in a group like the Zedwella war dragons have one dragon that is their leader. All the handlers agreed that the day would come when Morning Star would challenge the Dragon Master's dragon for the position to become the leader.

That night when he went home, Ty couldn't eat, he couldn't sleep and all he thought about was his dragon, Morning Star, being gone. No matter what his mother of father said about it going to be okay, he still worried.

"We just have to get him back," he told everybody he could. Every time he said it, Zac, his brother told him, "You'll do it. You can do anything."

"You just want to go on a ride on him." Ty retorted, but he was happy for his brother's support.

Ty Catches a Dragon

The next morning, Lord Alfred was waiting when Ty got to the cave, Blazing Comet was harnessed and ready to go.

"The Star Warriors were out this morning as the sun came up looking for the dragons," He said. "I was hoping they would still be alone. The Star Warriors found nothing, but will still keep looking."

"Think they hooked up with a group of other dragons?" Ogden asked.

"Most likely," the lord said.

"That's bad?" asked Ty.

"It makes things more difficult. We can't go after them while they are with a colony of other dragons. If we flew in with the war dragons, like we did when we were hunting, Morning Star would fly away with the rest of them. Also, while they are in the colony, they are protected by the other dragons.

"That means we have to wait for them to leave the colony pretty much by themselves," Ogden said, "and that's not likely,"

"They need to fly, don't they," Ty asked, to hunt for food?"

"Yes, but will they do it by themselves? Ogden said. "That's the tricky part. If they are with other dragons, then there will be a fight.

"And if we took more star warriors" Lord Alfred added, "they would see us and it would scare them off."

Ty Catches a Dragon

Ty looked lost. It looked hopeless.

"Don't be too down," Lord Alfred said as he put his hand on Ty's shoulder. "I've done this before. They don't have to be totally alone. Blazing Star can handle three or four wild dragons, so not all is lost.

**

Just before the sun rose to its highest point, they climbed up the side of a mountain, not far from a colony of wild dragons.

Blazing Star was hidden behind a rocky ridge which was easy to get back to if they had too.

It was the third colony they spied on so far. They watched the last two colonies for most of the morning, finding no sign of Morning Star or the female dragon.

"It's a big colony," Ogden observed as they came to a place where they could watch without being seen.

"Then we'll have to watch for a while longer here than at the other sites," Lord Alfred replied.

There was a lot of activity. Dragons were flying in and out of the site in groups. Some were returning with food for new young dragons who weren't old enough to fly.

"Keep your eye on the ones returning with game to eat." Lord Alfred said. "Our dragons are accustomed to being fed. They haven't learned how to go out by themselves and hunt for something to eat."

"That makes a difference?" Ty asked.

"It's bound to start a ruckus. The older dragons won't like it." the lord said. "With any luck, they will drive them off --make them look for their own food."

Ty Catches a Dragon

"There look," Ogen suddenly said. "Look over there at the other side."

"Yes, I see it," Lord Alfred said in a low slow voice as a smile crossed his face.

There was a fight happening on the other side of the colony area. A big female dragon flew in with the carcass of a deer. Her young ones were waiting for their meal. The female held the deer down with one foot and was pulling hunks of meat off with her beak throwing meat to the baby dragons.

Morning Star came in scattered the young about and grabbed a piece of meat that had fallen on the ground. He stood back waiting for more when the female attacked him. Spreading her wings, she jumped up and with her sharp talons extended, raked him across the chest.

Dragon fight Lineart
by c3d3-Canis on DeviantArt

Morning Star screamed in pain and jumped back, only to face a stream of flame. He screeched, as the mother dragon continued to attack him. She was in rage, wanting to kill him. She was protecting her young.

"We're in luck," Lord Alfred shouted

enthusiastically. "She'll drive him out of the colony,"

The Mother dragon's attack continued; Morning Star kept backing away. She was relentless--not about to stop. Morning Star started flapping his wings rising to get away from her.

"Hurry," Lord Alfred said. "He's going to be leaving soon. She's not going to stop until he leaves. "We have to get back to Blazing Comet and be ready to follow him."

The three turned and ran to get back to the waiting dragon.

As Morning Star took to the air, the dragon he escaped with from Parkerwella took flight and followed him.

They were hardly seated on Blazing Star when Lord Alfred commanded the dragon to rise and fly. As they flew up over the top of the ridge, they could see Morning Star in the distance. Not far behind him was the Zedwella female dragon he escaped with. Lord Alfred spurred his dragon to fly harder and catch them.

One of the colony's guard dragons watching from a nearby cliff, seeing Blazing Comet as an intruder, launched and made an attack.

Lord Alfred commanded Blazing Com-

et to fly into a climb and roll coming in behind the guard dragon. As he leveled out
he threw a long burst of flame. The blast
of fire caught the guard dragon's wing. It
burst into flame and the dragon went into a
spiral heading toward the ground.

"Hurry," Ogden yelled as he pointed to
the two dragons almost out of sight.

Again Lord Alfred commanded Blazing
Comet to fly after them. As a trained war
dragon, she knew just what was needed,
In a fearsom burst of energy she put all her
might into her wings and soon they were
starting to catch up.

"We're gaining on them," Ogden shouted as they started to close on Morning Star.

"Hang on," Lord Alfred shouted. "This
may be a bit tricky." He flew in above the
female and forced her to fly lower,

"Why her, and not "Morning Star," Ty shouted. "He'll get away."

"He won't leave her," the lord shouted back. "He'll find someplace close to land and watch."

Lower and lower the female flew until they came to another flat plateau where Blazing Comet, the larger dragon forced her to land. After they landed, the female threw a burst of flame toward them. Blazing Comet fired back, singing her. Past training by the Zedwella dragon trainers paid off. The female stopped in Blaing Comet's presence and stood still, waiting. She was under control again.

Ogden fastened a harness around her and mounted for the flight back.

"Wait. Let see what happens," Lord Alfred said with a wink Ty couldn't see.

Ty Catches a Dragon

Morning Star, just as Lord Alfred said, was watching them, perched on a rocky over looking the plateau they were on.

"Go over to that rise," he pointed toward it, "the one not to far from him." The lord handed him a heavy bag. 'Raw meat," he replied to Ty's curious glance. Remeber, Morning Star likes his meat, and I think he may be hungry by now. Maybe he'll listen to you now.

Ty slung the bag over his shoulder and climbed the rise.

"Morning Star," Ty called. "I've go something for you,"

The dragon looked at him, doing nothing in response.

"I've got your meat," Ty called as he threw a piece into the air. It landed on the ground not far away."

Throw a couple as far from you as you can," Lord Alfred shouted. "Get him to pick those up and he will follow the trail ."

Ty Catches a Dragon

Ty followed the lord's directions. The dragon, doing nothing, just stood there watching him,

"Come on boy. Come and get it. " Ty called as he reached into his bag. The meat was almost gone.

The drgon moved his head up and down, then side to side taking in the smell of the meat. He was hungry.

"Come on Morning Star," Ty called again, fear setting in. What if the dragon had turned wild again and wanted to stay that way.

Slowly Morning star jumped off the ledge, spread his wings and sailed down to the furthest piece of meat. He stopped, sniffed it than scooped it up swallowing in one bite. He looked up at the next piece, a little closer to Ty and took a couple of steps toward it, looked at Ty and scooped it up too.

"Good Boy," Ty encouraged him. "come get some more."

Slowly, the dragon came forward, eating each piece as it came.

When the meat was gone, Ty commanded. "Stop"

Morning Star stopped.

"Stay," Ty said as he walked around the beast.

The climbing strap and harness were still on it. Ty slowly took hold of the rope and pulled himself up unto Morning Star's back. The dragon, on command to stay, didn't move.

"He's okay," Ty called to the others.

Lord Alfred climbed up on Blazing

Comet, and called to Ty and Ogden. "Let's go home."

Just before sunset they arrived back in Parkerwella at the dragon cave to chears. Even the handler who Morning Star gave same so much trouble to cheered. He was happy for Ty.

The next day the Dragon Master and Lord Alfred were waiting for Ty when he arrived."

"We've go a problem," the Dragon Master said. "Your dragon's had a taste of the wild again. He's likely to want to go again."

"But, there is something we can do about it."Lord Alfred added.

"Yes," Ty said as he waited.

"We think it's time for him to become a war dragon," the Dragon Master said, "He needs the extra training and discipline.

"A war dragon," Ty said slowly. "You're going to make him a war dragon now?" Fear crept across his face. If Morning Star was a war dragon he would be assigned to a Star Warrior.

"I think so," the Dragon Master said with a smile on his face. "It's time."

Ty stood bravely, "Okay," he said. "It was our agreement. Who is he going to be given too." He held back a tear.

The Dragon Master and Lord Alfred burst out laughing.

Ty Catches a Dragon

"You," Lord Alfred laughed. "If he doesnt' get more training, he will probably try to take off again. He needs more. disipline to be a war dragon. It will make him more responsive and less likely to run again.

"So," said the Dragon Master, "since you are his trainer, you will have to be trained as a Star Warrior too."

"Wow," Ty responded. "Me a star warrior?"

"Trained as a Star Warrior," the Dragon Master said. "It will be many years before you become one. But there is no harm in learning a little early."

He looked over at Lord Alfred, "Don't you agree."

Lord Alfred just nodded his head and laughed.

Everyday, as soon as school let out, Ty ran through the woods to Morning Star's cave and they would go flying. They flew out over the mountains, and often great distances until the sun set. Morning Star continued to grow and became very strong. He responded to Ty's slightest command asd they became a team.

"Time to make him a war dragon," Lord Asfred said one day as Ty came into the dragon cave to take Morning Star for his daily exercise.

"Let's take a ride," Lord Alfred said as Ogen brought Blazing Star out, harnessed up and ready to fly.

Ty Catches a Dragon

"You're in for a treat today," Ogden told Ty. "Just hang on tight."

Before, Ty had ridden with Ogden to give the beast his exercise. The flights were enjoyable, cruising out over the mountains in the late afternoon before sunsets.

Ty climbed up in back of Lord Alfred.

"Hang on," the lord commanded Ty.

"Raise Up," he shouted and rapped Blazing Comet on the side of the neck with is staff.

The dragon got to its feet, rose up into the air, roared a mighty roar and blew a stream of flame toward the cave entrance.

"Fly." Lord Alfred commanded as he slapped the dragon against the front of his leg with the staff. With a downward burst of her wings, another mighty roar, and the dragon launched into the air and out the cave entrance.

As they sailed out over the mountains, Lord Alfred commanded the drgon to fly faster and faster. Soon they were moving faster than Ty ever though a dragon could fly. Over mountain range after mountain range, Blazing Star, not getting tired, flew without slowing down.

"Hold on," Lord Alfred shouted as a re-minder. Suddenly, Blazing Comet cleared a mountain top and went into a dive, like an arrow shot hign and was falling faster and faster toward the valley below.

"See those three big trees sitting all alone," Lord Alfred shouted as he pointed his staff at it."

"Yes, I think so," Ty called back.

"Watch them." the lord shouted.

dive, and drove him to fly as hard as he could toward the trees. The dragon roared a fearsome battle cry. As a trained war beast, she lived for the battle. To fight an enemy was the meaning of life, and Blazing Comet put everyting she had into it.

She was on an attack command, and threw an immense stream of fire at the firest tree which burst into flames as she flew just over the top of it. With a mighty burst of her wings, she turned straight up, climbing faster and faster.

Half way back up the mountain side Lord Alfred turned her and put her into another dive, this time moving faster than they had before and aimed straight down at the second tree. As she grew closer, Blazing Comet threw a long stream of flame hitting the tree. As they pulled up, Ty could feel the heat of the flames as the tree burst into flame just under them.

Then the lord pulled the dragon around in a circle. Keeping it tight, Blazing Comet leaned sideways and with the dragon still flying sideways came out of the circle fired another stream of fame and the last tree burst into flame.

With the maneuver complete, the loard brought his dragon up to the top of the mountain peaks flying so they could look down at the three smoldering trees.

"Now," he shouted to Ty. "That is what you need to teach Morning Star to do."

The next day Lord Alfred told Ty it was his turn. They took Morning Star out, Ty flew with the lord on the back giving him instructions.

"Slowly," Lord Alfred continued to say. Do it right, then learn to do it fast. It's no good being fast if you miss."

As time continued, Lord Alfred taught Ty how to handle a dragon like a warrior, flying between the mountains so the enemy couldn't tell where you were, then skim over the top of a mountain peak and nose diving down the other side to make a surprise attacks. He learned to do aerial maneuvers with Morning Star like they were fighting another dragon in the sky. Lord Alfred told him to practice these maneuvers by himself and later they would learn to fly in formation along with the war dragons of Zedwella to learn to be a part of its fighting force

Ty and Morning Star practiced hard. Ty wanted his dragon to be the best. He knew Morning Star wanted it too. Every few days, Lord Alfred would come along to see how Ty was doing and to give him tips and instruction for improvement.

At the turn of each moon, the Dragon Master would ride with Ty to see how he was coming along. He was very happy, claiming that Ty was doing a great job and Morning Star was turning into a great war dragon. Now it is work, work, work, but I know you are up to it."

"Today is the king's birthday," Ty said to his family at breakfast. You have to come. There is to be a big celebration with a big parade. The War Dragons are going to be there and Morning Star and I are going to be in it." He finished his breakfast before anyone else and hurried out of the house to the dragon cave.

"You've got to be on your best behavior," Ty said to Morning Star as they lined up for the parade. I want everyone to be proud of you."

Lord Alfred came up riding Blazing Comet. "You understand what we are going to do?"

"Yep, we parade down the main street for everyone to see then go to the field behind the palace and wait for the people to gather. Then we will take off and fly in formation over the town and land back on the field in front of the king's stand."

"Yes, it's an opportunity for the people to get close to the dragons and see them."

The parade worked out as planned. The dragons came down the main street to the cheering of the people and on to the field behind the palace. Upon a signal from the Dragon Master, the lead dragon leaped into the air and flew away followed by the rest of the dragons. Ty was with them next to Lord Alfred.

They landed in formation in front of the king who stood up and applauded. The Dragon Master, standing next to him, called. "Will Lord Alfred and Ty come forward."

"What," Ty said.

"Come," Lord Alfred said as he an Ty

spurred their dragons ahead of the rest of the formation.

They stopped in front of the king,

In a formal voice for all to hear, the Dragon Master said to the king, "Sir, I would like to introduce you to young master Ty and his noble dragon Morning Star. He is our youngest trainer and has done a wonderful job training his dragon. One day it will be a great war dragon for your kingdom"

The king clapped. "Congratulations, young master Ty, you have done well. Your dragon is a noble warrior. Upon the Dragon Master's recommendation, I am announcing, for all the people in the land to hear, that you are officially a Dragon Trainer in the Kingdom of Zedwella."

The End

Ty Catches a Dragon

Meet the Author

Donald W Frederickson

Mr. Frederickson is an exciting new author in the writing world.   In the last three years he has published two new novels, written numerous short stories, gained considerable notoriety in local literary circles with his epic Viking poetry and produced a trilogy of children's books written for his grandsn who wants to be a "dragon trainer".

Mr. Frederickson has traveled extensively, providing experiences from which he draws liberally in his writing.   He lived a year and a half in Eritrea, Africa during his military service, toured Europe with a backpack in the Sixties, and has taken many extensive trips into Mexico and Central America. He holds an undergraduate degree in Anthropology which promoted his love for archaeology.   His extensive travel in Mexico and Guatemala, visiting over thirty arcaeological sites, remnants from the the Maya civilization, has led him to write "The Warrior Prince", an historical fiction novel on one of the last great Maya warrior kings.

Retiring over ten years ago from an industrial executive position, Mr. Frederickson now spends his time traveling, writing and providing presentations on the Maya culture to libraries, museums and academic institutions.

Made in the USA
Columbia, SC
24 May 2018